MR. SLOW
Rolls On

Roger Hargreaves

MR. MEN   **LITTLE MISS**

MR. MEN™ LITTLE MISS™ © THOIP (a Sanrio company)

Mr Slow Rolls On © 2014 THOIP (a Sanrio company)
Printed and published under licence from Price Stern Sloan, Inc., Los Angeles.
First published in France in 1997 by Hachette Livre
This edition published in 2014 by Dean, an imprint of Egmont UK Limited,
The Yellow Building, 1 Nicholas Road, London W11 4AN

ISBN 978 0 6035 6997 5
58237/1
Printed in Great Britain

EGMONT

Engines were revving, horns were blaring, a crowd was cheering.

What a din!

What do you think was going on?

Little Miss Bossy had organised a road race and all the competitors were waiting at the starting line.

"… And here we have Mr Clever," announced Little Miss Bossy.

Mr Clever was indeed very clever. He had found a way to travel high above all the exhaust fumes of the other cars!

With his latest invention, the super-duper-elevated-highview-speedomatic-autocar, that problem was solved!

"And behind him," continued Little Miss Bossy, "is Mr Silly with his most unusual car. A car with square wheels!"

"And finally," Little Miss Bossy announced, smiling to herself, "here is Mr Slow driving a steamroller! Not the fastest choice! Hurry up Mr Slow, the race is about to begin."

And with that, she waved her flag and they were off.

Mr Uppity overtook all the other drivers in his big, powerful limousine.

He arrived at a junction and …

… turned the sign around.

Now the arrow showing the drivers which way to go was pointing in the wrong direction.

Do you think all the other drivers went the wrong way?

That's certainly what Mr Uppity hoped would happen.

But no, not at all. Mr Uppity had forgotten that Mr Clever was indeed very clever and that from his high car he could see the finishing line in the distance.

"Somebody has turned the sign around," he called out at the junction. "This is the right way to go. Follow me!"

And far behind them all, Mr Slow followed his friends … slowly … on his steamroller.

He was in no hurry at all.

He was just happy to be joining in.

Further along the course a local farmer was selling potatoes by the side of the road.

"Beautiful potatoes! Buy my beautiful potatoes!" he called out.

Hmmm, do you think Little Miss Naughty has come to buy potatoes?

Certainly not!

She has come to cause trouble!

Soon the poor farmer was buried under a huge pile of potatoes. There were potatoes everywhere. And of course the potatoes had rolled all over the road.

"Danger! Potatoes on the road!" cried Little Miss Naughty as Mr Uppity drove up.

"Clear the road at once," demanded Mr Uppity.

"That's out of the question, Mr Uppity," said Little Miss Naughty. "You'll just have to wait."

It wasn't long before everyone in the race was queued up behind Mr Uppity and the potato blockage.

Eventually Mr Slow arrived on his steamroller and …

… slowly he drove over the potatoes and

… slowly he took the lead in the race!

"I'm sorry," called Mr Slow to the farmer, as he drove by. "I seem to have caused quite a mess!"

"Never mind," replied the farmer cheerfully. "Mashed potato for sale. Beautiful mashed potato for sale!"

And just around the corner from all the mashed potato, a cheering crowd had gathered.

It was the finishing line and who was crossing it?

It was none other than Mr Slow!

What a brilliant performance!

What a winner!

Little Miss Sunshine had the honour of giving Mr Slow his award.

The crowd cheered and cheered.

"But if Mr Slow is the winner," said Mr Nosey, "he can't be as slow as everybody thinks. We'll have to call him Mr Not-So-Slow!"

And everyone agreed.

And as for Mr Uppity, well …

He now hates mashed potato!